DRAFT 1
MACK VS MENTAL INSTIUTION
PART 2
WHAT HAVE I GOT IN THE MIDDLE OF?
I0713653

IT WAS SOME TIME LATER. MACK WAS NOW SITTING BACK
IN HIS CELL

HIS EYES LOOKED SLIGHTLY MORE FOCUSED, LIKE HE
WAS MORE AWAKE

HE LOOKED DOWN AND THREW THE CARD
ON THE FLOOR

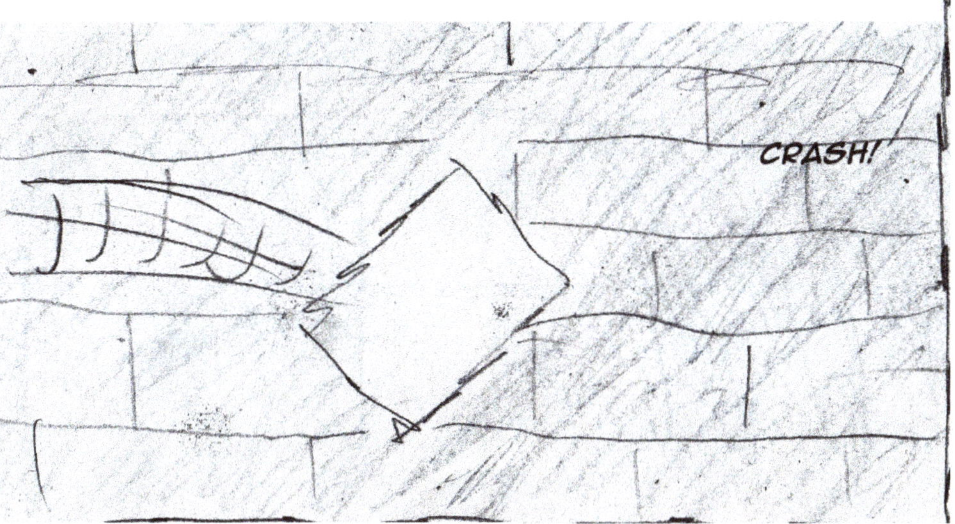

CRASH!

IT LANDED ON THE
FLOOR AS HE SAID
"THERE'S NO POINT"

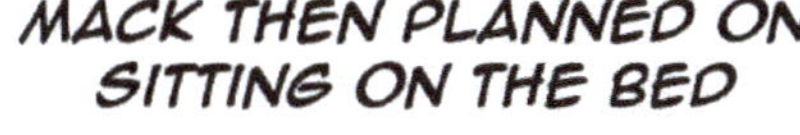

CALL
(555) 113-4567

MACK THEN PLANNED ON
SITTING ON THE BED

HE CONTINUED SITTING THERE, LOOKING DEPRESSED........THAT WAS UNTIL SUDDENLY.....

A DOOR SWUNG OPEN!

SLAM!

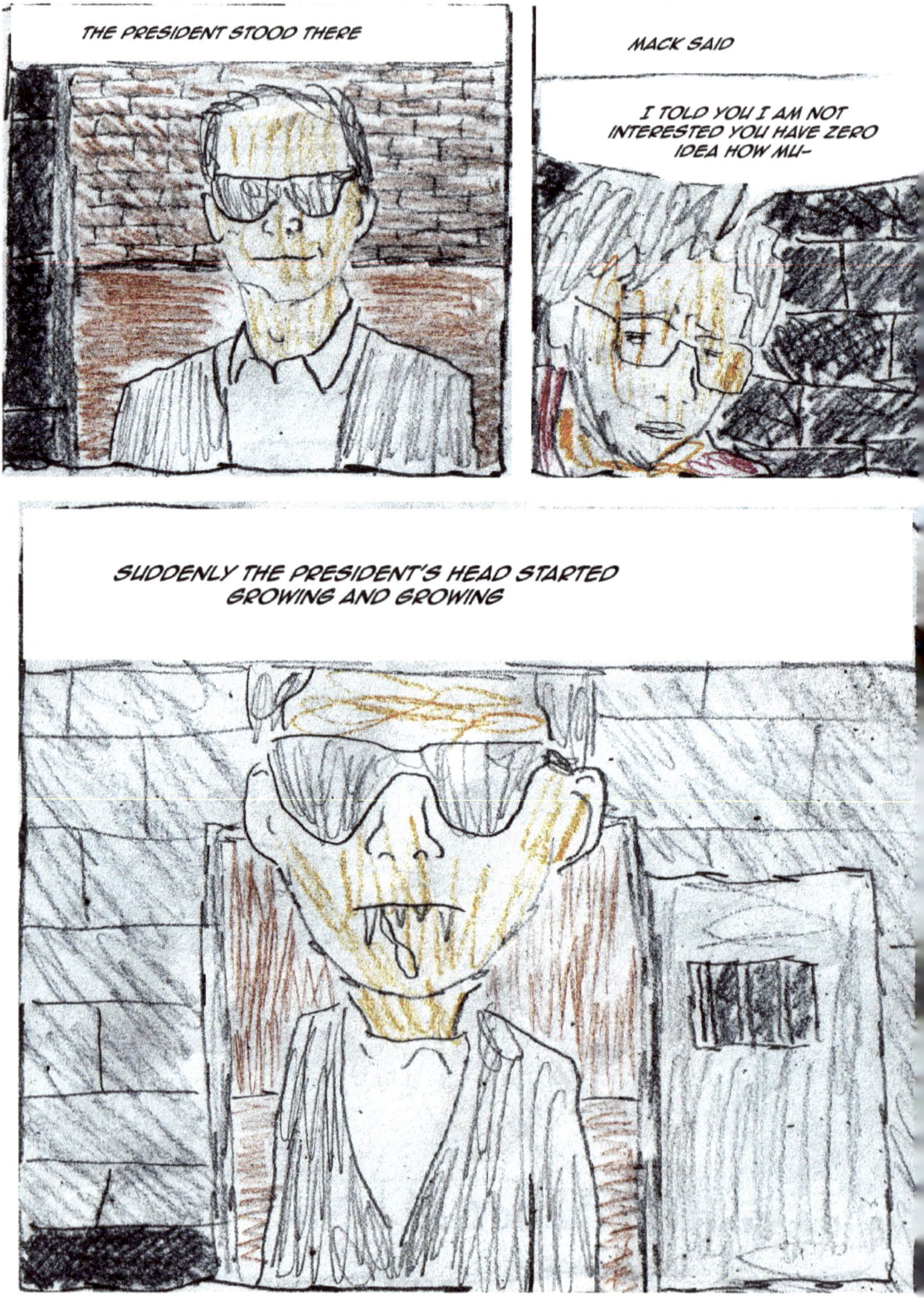

THE PRESIDENT STOOD THERE

MACK SAID
I TOLD YOU I AM NOT INTERESTED YOU HAVE ZERO IDEA HOW MU-

SUDDENLY THE PRESIDENT'S HEAD STARTED GROWING AND GROWING

MACK STOOD BACK! HIS BACK CRASHED AGAINST THE WALL!!!

THE PRESIDENT SAID

JOOOOOOOOOOOOOOIN MEEEEEEEEEEEEEEEEEEEEEE!!!!!!!!!!!!!!!!!!!!!!

LOT'S OF TONGS SLID OUT HIS MOUTH!!!!!!!!!

MACK THEN WOKE UP!!!!

MACK REALIZED IT WAS
ANOTHER NIGHTMARE!!!!!

HE THOUGHT THE PRESIDENT HAD SHOWN HIM KINDNESS BUT IT WAS
JUST ANOTHER NIGHTMARE, HE THOUGHT TO HIMSELF HE SHOULD BE
USED TO IT BY NOW EVERY GLIMMER OF HOPE HE SUBCONSCIOUSLY
CLUNG TO HAD ALWAYS PROVED IN VAIN!

NO, I NEED TO STOP HAVING HOPE, I NEED, I'M GOING TO GET OUT OF HERE, I'LL FIND THE PRESIDENT IS NOT REAL, THEN I'LL FINALLY BE ABLE TO ACCEPT........THAT IGHT......IS JUST A MYTH AND DOES NOT EXIST

SO, WITH THAT MACK SAW THE PRISON BARS ON THE DOOR! HE THEN LOOKED AT THE KEYHOLE!

SOMEONE GAVE HIM SOUP!

HE THEN QUIETLY POURED SOUP IN THE KEYHOLE

IT WOULD TAKE MONTHS TO GRADUALLY MELT THE METAL SO HE COULD BREAK IT OPEN, BUT EVEN THEN ALL THE GUARDS WOULD JUST SWARM HIM, BUT THERE WAS NO OTHER WAY, OR WAS THERE?

MACK HAD A SECRET WEAPON IN HIS GLASSES! IT WAS A TINY SIM CARD JUST ABOVE THE EAR BUT WAS USELESS WITHOUT A COMPUTER

.......BUT THEN MACK TOOK HIS GLASSES OFF AND PICKED THE SIM CARD OUT

HE THEN PLUGGED IT IN THE RIGHT EYE OF HIS GLASSES!!!!

SUDDENLY HIS GLASSES LIT UP! SHOWING HIM EVERYTHING!

HE WAS ABLE TO CONTACT IS SECRET BASE IN FRANCE...............IN AN ALTERNATE DIMENSION.

DISTRESS
SIGNAL
DETECTED

SUDDENLY A SUIT VANISHED!!!!!!

MACK STOOD THERE WITH HIS ARMS OUT READY FOR IT TO APPEAR IN FRONT OF HIM! AND LATCH ON TO HIS BODY

THE GROUND SHOOK OF THIS UNIVERSE 2-0-1-5. (THE BASE HIDDEN
UNDER THE RED CAFÉ WAS WHERE THE SUIT HAS TELEPORTED AWAY
SENDING SHOCKWAVES THROUGH THE TECTONIC PLATES)

IT THEN TELEPORTED IN FRONT OF HIM....BUT OUTSIDE THE CELL DOOR.....

MACK'S EYES LOOKED SHOCKED! HE CAME TO THE BARS OF THE DOOR AND LOOKED AT THE SUIT, JUST OUT OF REACH

AS HE SAW THE SUIT OUTSIDE IN THE T POSITION

AN ALARM WAS GOING OFF!!!!

SUDDENLY AN A.R.C SECURITY GUARD WAS RUNNING DOWN THE CORRIDOR!!!!!!!!
STOP IN THE NAME OF THE A.R.C!!!!!
BEEP!
BEEP!
BEEP!
BEEP!

HE ACTIVATED THE ELECTRICITY IN HIS GLOVE!!!!!
BEEP!
BEEP!
BEEP!
BEEP!
DON'T WORRY! THIS WILL ONLY HURT ALOT!!!!

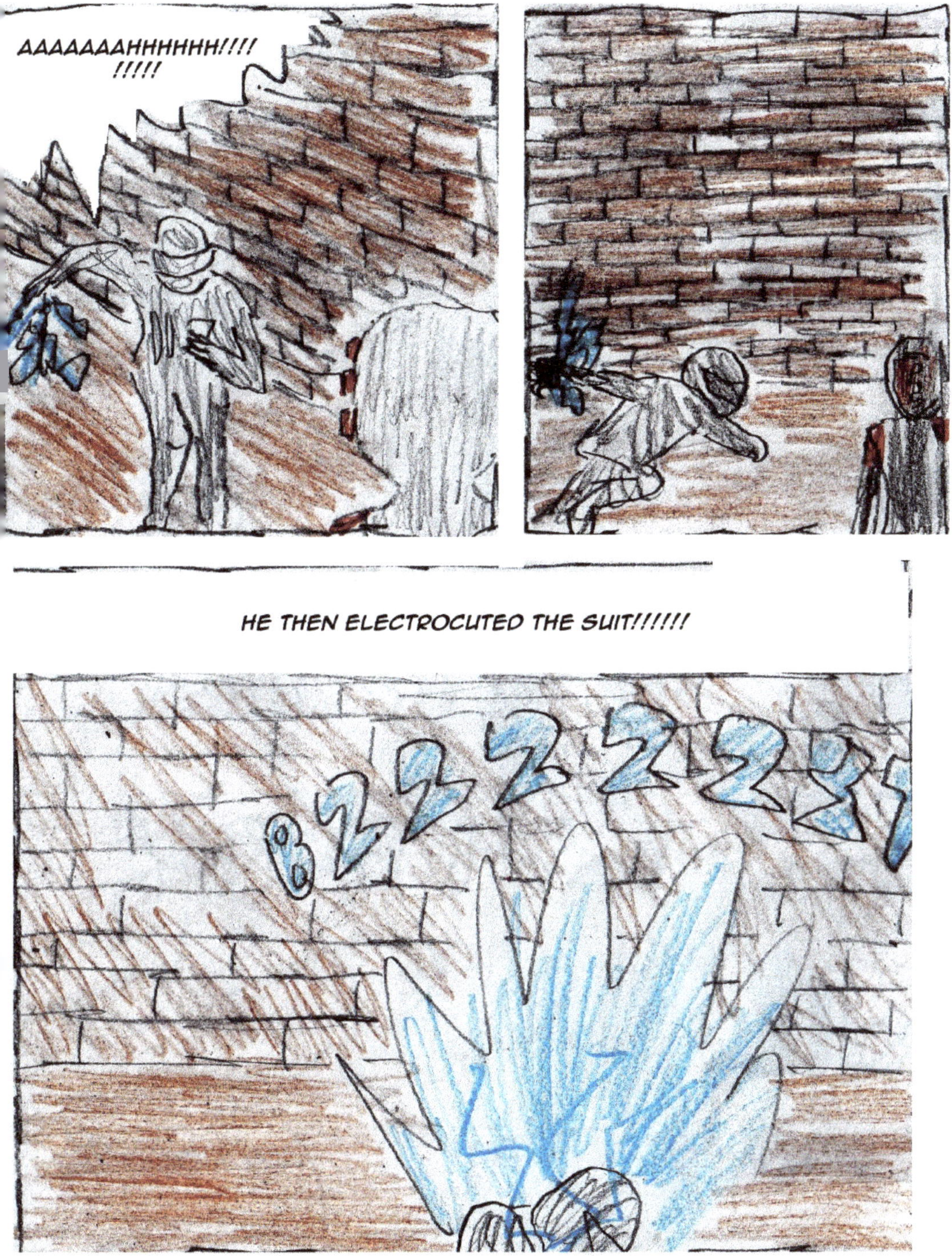

HE THEN ELECTROCUTED THE SUIT!!!!!!

MEANWHILE MACK WAS SUDDENLY LOOKING VERY HAPPY AND EXCITED. HE WAS HAPPY BECAUSE HIS DEPRESSION WAS ABOUT TO END

HE HAPPILY MADE HIMSELF A NOOSE OUT OF THE BED SHEETS

AND HAD A HAPPY GRIN ON HIS FACE AS HE TIED IT TO THE LIGHTBULB ABOVE

HE MOVED THE BED TO THE MIDDLE OF THE ROOM
WHILE HUMMING TO HIMSELF

AND TOOK AN ENTHUSIASTIC STEP UP ONTO THE BED AND PUT
THE NOOSE AROUND HIS NECK

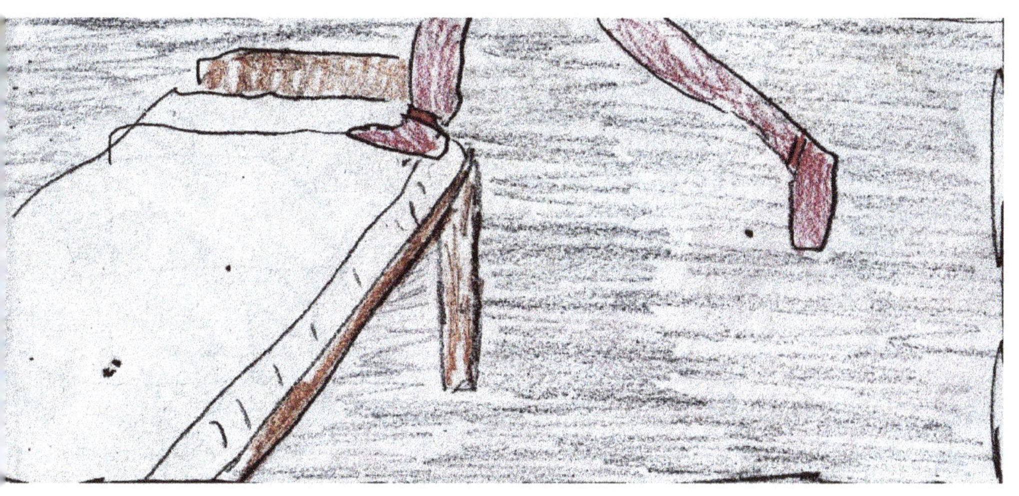

THE SECURITY GUARD LOOKED THROUGH THE DOOR

HE SAID
AW CRAP

THE A.R.C GUARD SAID
FALL BACK, WE'VE GOT ANOTHER SUICIDE
... ...
AGAIN

THE A.R.C OPENED THE DOOR
HE SAID

SUDDENLY MACK JUMPED DOWN! (HE WAS HOLDING ON TO THE ROPE PRETENDING TO HAVE HUNG HIMSELF)

WHAT THE F—
THU

THE A.R.C FELL TO THE GROUND KNOCKED OUT

MACK QUICKLY GOT IN THE T POSITION

THE SUIT LATCHED ON TO HIM

THE SECURITY GUARDS HID BEHIND THE DOCTOR

SCANNING COMPLETE, IT'S A SUIT FROM ANOTHER UNIVERSE

WE SHOULD PROBABLY START RUNNING

MACK THEN SAID

TELEPORTATION ACTIVATE!

THE SUIT THEN SAID "THIS SUIT REQUIRES AN UPDATE, PLEASE DOWNLOAD THE UPDATE BEFORE CONTINUING"

....
CURSE YOU
ASHLEIGH
....
CURSE YOU AND
YOUR UPDATES

MORE AND MORE PEOPLE WERE COMING DOWN THE
CORRIDOR CHARGING!!!!!

SUDDENLY THE PEOPLE RAN INTO THE ROOM

THE ESSENTIAL SUIT WAS ON THE FLOOR KNOCKED OUT

THE A.R.C GUARD APPARENTLY STOOD THERE SAYING

HE HUNG HIMSELF, THEM CAME BACK TO LIFE THEN I
STOPPED HIM THERE WAS NOTHING I COULD DO

THE A.R.C GUARD WAS RUNNING DOWN THE CORRIDOR!!!!!!!!!!

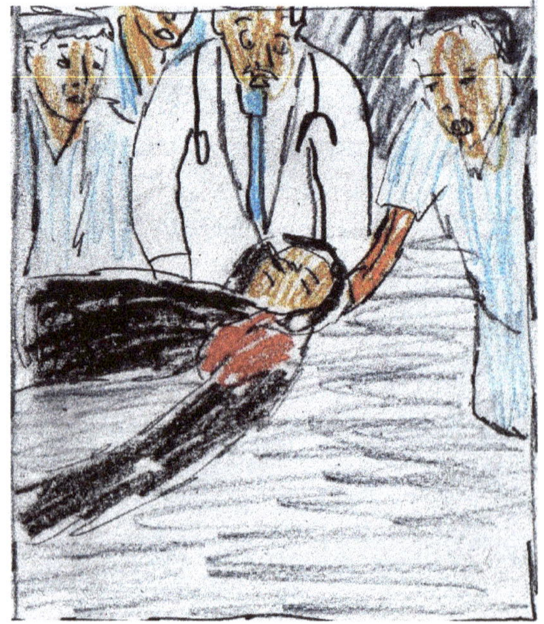

THE GUARDS IN THE ROOM ROLLED THE ESSENTIAL SUIT OVER

TO REVEAL IT WAS THE A.R.C GUARD IN THE ESSENTIAL SUIT!!!!!!!!
MACK HAS SWAPPED THE COSTUMES!!!!!!!!!!!!!!

HE WAS RUNNING THROUGH THE CORRIDOR DRESSED AS AN A.R.C AGENT!!!!!!!!!!!!!!
HUFF HUFF
HUFF HUFF
HUFF HUFF
HUFF HUFF
HUFF HUFF
HUFF HUFF
HUFF HUFF
HUFF

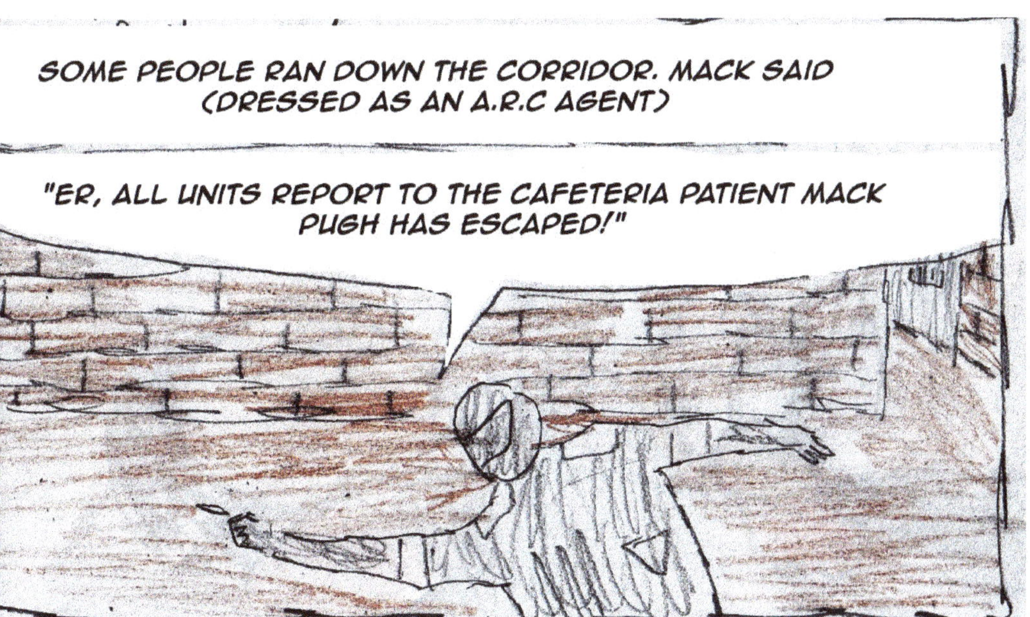

SOME PEOPLE RAN DOWN THE CORRIDOR. MACK SAID (DRESSED AS AN A.R.C AGENT)
"ER, ALL UNITS REPORT TO THE CAFETERIA PATIENT MACK PUGH HAS ESCAPED!"

THE GUARD SAID

"ROGER THAT!"

MACK THEN KEPT RUNNING

HUFF HUFF
HUFF HUFF
HUFF
FOR CHRISTMAS I
WOULD LIKE A CAR

MACK WAS RUNNING AND
RUNNING UNTIL SUDDENLY....

HE SLIPPED ON A WET FLOOR!!!!!!

HE THEN FELL OVER!!!!!!
CRASH!

HE QUICKLY STOOD BACK UP!!!!!!!!!!!!!!!!!!!!!!

ATTENTION ALL UNITS MACK PUGH HAS ESCAPED CUSTODY AND IS POSING AS A.R.C AGENT 7-8-1 MAX EMMONS!

MACK SAW THE EMERGENCY DOORS SHUTTING!!!!